D1097942

LITTLE NAVAJO BLUEBIRD

ALSO BY ANN NOLAN CLARK

IN MY MOTHER'S HOUSE
MAGIC MONEY
LOOKING-FOR-SOMETHING
SECRET OF THE ANDES
BLUE CANYON HORSE
SANTIAGO
THIRD MONKEY
A SANTO FOR PASQUALITA
WORLD SONG

LITTLE *Navajo* BLUEBIRD

STORY BY ANN NOLAN CLARK

ILLUSTRATED BY PAUL LANTZ

THE VIKING PRESS · NEW YORK

FIRST PUBLISHED APRIL 1943

SECOND PRINTING MARCH 1945

THIRD PRINTING OCTOBER 1947

FOURTH PRINTING OCTOBER 1948

FIFTH PRINTING NOVEMBER 1951

SIXTH PRINTING DECEMBER 1953

SEVENTH PRINTING MARCH 1957

EIGHTH PRINTING APRIL 1960

CONTENTS

I. THE TRADING POST

Doli peeped shyly from the deep folds of her mother's wide skirts. Her black eyes shone.

Here was no home hogan, no rounded mud-plastered walls, no friendly center fire on which the supper mutton stew slowly bubbled and steamed. This place was the

Trading Post, a great room of boarded walls with corners. The walls were lined with ladderlike shelves filled with hard things and soft things. At one end were Navajo blankets of many numbers, folded and stacked in piles of colors. On the side in back of the counter were cans on cans of foods. Some of the cans were covered with papers the colors of sunset and others were beautiful with pictures of green growing things.

Doli's mouth watered for the good food the cans held, she could almost taste their goodness.

Father was looking at the glass case full of silver rings and bracelets, coral and shell necklaces, and strings of turquoise. Father stood there, not talking, not moving, just looking at those things within the case.

Mother had come to the Post to sell a blanket of her weaving and to buy cans of tomatoes and peaches, sacks of wheat flour and cane sugar, bags of salt and coffee. If the day was a lucky one and Mother received many of the round, silver money pieces for her blanket, she would buy more things, perhaps candy, lard, baking powder.

Doli could not remember that she had been to this Trading Post before, although her mother said she had. Hobah, the elder sister, had told her of it many times as they sat together in the shade of the twisted juniper and lazily watched Sun-Carrier going on his day-long journey through the blue above them.

Doli was afraid, but very curious. Soon she ventured out from the shelter of her mother's many skirts and found a better place between the knees of her tall father where he stood looking at the turquoise and silver.

She leaned far out from the gateway of his knees, her stiffly gathered yellow-brown calico skirts petaled flower-like above her bare brown feet. Turquoise earbobs swung gently against her thin brown cheeks. Her velvet blouse was the color of a bluebird's wing, for she was a Bluebird child of the yellow sand country. Her thick black hair was smoothed back in a fat queue and tied with strings of white yarn, for she was a woman child and must look and act like Mother and like Elder Sister, Hobah.

Doli thought to herself, "This is a great place, this Trading Post." Her heart sang, "Beautiful. Beautiful. Things here are beautiful."

Flies buzzed in and out the doorway. Mother looked at many things and marked in her mind those it was good that she should buy. Doli watched her mother as she bought, one by one, the things she needed.

Through the open door she could see Navajo men squatting in the sand. Slowly, slowly, step by step, Doli went over to see what they were doing. They were playing a game. They drew a circle in the sand and placed small stones around its line. Two sticks made a little door in the circle of stones. Doli peeked around the side of the Trading Post door. There was Uncle! He was playing with the other men. He had three chips which were painted black on one side. Uncle tossed the chips and they came down with the unpainted side showing. That gave him one mark for each chip so he could place his little stick three stones from the door of the circle. The men spoke little. Their game was silent and swift. Doli liked watching them, but she was afraid to stay long for fear she might miss something else exciting.

She went around the wall, back to where her mother was buying things from the Trader's shelves and bins. Doli stood on tiptoe with her big eyes just above the counter. Mother's shopping was a game, too. Mother put a bag of cornmeal to one side and gave the Trader some silver pieces from the small pile which he had given her for the blanket. Mother waited a long time, looking and thinking. Then she put a box of matches beside the cornmeal and paid the Trader some more round money, this time a little piece.

Mother pulled her blanket closer about her. She went outside to the wagon to get another blanket in which to carry the things she bought. Doli went with her. They did not hurry. Going to the Trading Post was not an everyday happening. It was a day that had been looked forward to and planned for and it must be enjoyed slowly. Doli and her mother did not intend to treat it lightly or hurriedly. Buying things was fun enough and important enough to take a long time to finish.

They did not seem to be looking, but they saw the men who were still playing their game. Uncle was tossing the chips again. This time all the black sides came up. Each black chip gave three marks, so Uncle moved his little stick nine stones around the circle. Uncle was good at tossing chips. His little stick was way ahead. He was winning.

Mother went into the store to unfold her blanket on the counter and put into it her bundles and bags. This done, she bought a bag of coffee and looked longingly at some bright velvet.

Doli watched her father. He was not talking to the Trader. He was not looking at the Trader, but the Trader was looking at him. The Trader was looking at the new bracelet Father was wearing. Father had just finished it this morning before they had started for the Post. He had made it to sell, but now he acted as if he had forgotten that he had it. Doli looked up at him. His eyes were still. Suddenly she knew something. Father was playing a game, too. He was playing that he did not want to sell his bracelet.

The Trader was very busy. When he was not taking

round silver money from Mother's pile for the things she bought, he was trying to make Father want to sell his bracelet. Doli ducked her head. She had to put her hand over her mouth to hide a smile. At last Father said, Yes, he would sell the bracelet and the Trader gave him four round silver money pieces for it. Father took also, for good measure, some little brown papers and a bag of tobacco for the cigarettes which he liked to smoke.

The Trader gave Father a square of paper with black marks on it. He said it was a letter from Big Brother in the far-distant School land where he had gone so long ago. The Trader made the paper talk for Father, saying words of greeting from Big Brother to his home people.

Doli suddenly had a great longing for the home hogan and for tall, laughing Big Brother, who used to bring her gifts of bluebird feathers and colored stones. But that was long ago before he had gone to the School. Only once since then had he returned to visit them.

Doli took the candy which the Trader gave her, but the wonders of the Trading Post were gone. She no longer saw the cans of food, the blankets, the silver-trimmed saddles, the beautiful blue kettles and pans. She wanted to go home to her sheepskin bed by the friendly center fire. She was tired. She was hungry, so hungry that she could almost smell the hot, woolly smell of the supper mutton stew. She remembered the first supper with Big Brother the time he had come back to visit. There was mutton stew that night, but he had not eaten. He had sat in the shadows of the darkening hogan, not laughing, but quiet with a kind of anger that was frightening. When he spoke at all it was of a table and dishes and chairs and beds. Doli had not understood. What were these things of which he talked, she wondered. Why did he want them for this home place which always had felt so right?

Big Brother's second going had been in the season of the corn-growing-large. Corn-growing-large time had come again, but Big Brother had not returned.

Doli looked up. She had forgotten that she was here at the Trading Post. The Trader was looking down at her. He had given her candy. Father spoke to her in Navajo. He said in his low kind voice, "This White Man likes children, I think."

Little Bluebird pushed against her father's knees. In English she said to the Trader, "Big Brother." It was all the English she knew. Big Brother, himself, had taught her Navajo tongue to say it. "Big Brother," she repeated softly, shyly, but with great courage to show him that she was pleased with his gift of candy.

Tall Father moved toward the door. Doli went with him. He lifted her into the wagon and untied his horses from the bar. By and by Mother finished shopping and came out with her blanket bundle. She, too, climbed into the wagon. She pulled her blanket high up around her head and from within its shelter she looked out at the wagons and horses and people around the Trading Post. Doli pulled up her blanket but she, too, saw the happenings around her.

Navajos sitting in the door shade looked up from their game and nodded. Navajos standing by the watering trough looked back and nodded. Father said to them, "The People speak as they pass. My way lies in this direction."

It was sun-hot time of day. Far away a whirlwind danced across the sand. Doli held the bag of candy tightly in her thin brown hand. Father called to the horses a high-pitched, long-drawn "A-ya-an-na."

They started toward home. The horses moved slowly along the sandy ruts. Yucca bloomed by the side of the road. A road-runner ran a race with the wagon. A prairie dog sat by his front door and watched their passing. A jackrabbit loped across the road.

Father sang as he drove along. Doli was sleepy. Her head nodded to her father's singing and to the lurchings of the wagon.

It had been a long day. It had been a good day, but now the journey to the Trading Post was over.

II. THE HOGAN

Home hogan was a rounded, mud-plastered house with
a blanket-covered door facing eastward. There were no
windows. The chimney was a hole in the middle of the
rounded, mud-plastered roof. The floor was clean yellow
sand. Sheepskins were the beds; boxes were the chairs, and

18

the stove was a hollowed place in the sandy floor. A brushed-clean place beside the stove was used for table.

This was the family hogan, their house, their home, a friendly, happy place for Doli.

When Doli and her mother and her father reached home hogan from the Trading Post, day had come to cool time. Red rocks were sending out their long gray shadows to the edges of the sandwash near by.

Elder Sister, Hobah, had been out all day with the

flocks, but now she was home again. She had turned the sheep and the goats into the night corral among the piñons. She had carried water from the well. She had chopped wood at the woodpile and now smoke from the newly made supper fire filled the hogan door. Hobah was beautiful, tall for her age, slender, and strong. She did whatever work there was to do, quietly and well, as her mother had taught her.

Now she came out to the wagon to carry her mother's blanket bundle into the hogan. Mother went to milk the goats and Doli stumbled sleepily to sit on her sheepskin bed beside the fire. She told Hobah of the happenings of the day. She told her about Uncle's winning the game that he played with the men and about Father's selling the bracelet to the Trader. She told about the things she had done and had seen and had heard, but she did not say Big Brother's name. One said with words those things that the eyes saw, but even with Hobah one guarded the whisperings of the heart.

Father came in. He had unhitched his horses and had hobbled them for the night grazing. Hobah hastened to serve him with food. Mother's blanket had been full of good things. Tonight the family had store bread and canned peaches to eat with the mutton stew. Tonight the strong black coffee was sweetened with sugar and colored creamy brown with milk from a can.

Fiery clouds of sunset covered the sky and changed the yellow sands of the drywash to purple and rose. Hobah moved quietly about the hogan, serving Father with food and helping Mother end the work of the day.

Doli was sleepy but not yet was she ready to let sleep come. She sat in the door of the hogan and let the little night winds wash her face with their cooling fingers. Far away, far off, in the thickening shadows, she heard singing. Some stranger singing. At first it was just a singing sound, but little by little, as the rider came nearer, the singing sound grew into words of song, into words of the hogan song. Clearly they came across the gray shadows, the words of the hogan song:

"My hogan,
  My hogan,
  My happy hogan,
  My blessed hogan,
  Hogan.
  My hogan."

So sang the far rider as he urged his tired horse homeward.

Father came to stand in the hogan doorway. He took up the chant. He sent his singing out into the coming night to meet the tired rider to sing him home. Father sang:

"Look!
  Yonder the hogan,
  The beautiful hogan,
  The precious hogan."

Doli gathered her skirts close around her. She hugged her knees in delight. Father's singing wrapped her in a blanket of happiness.

"My hogan,
  Hogan,"

sang Father, and the rider answered:

"Hogan beautiful,
  My hogan."

Doli turned toward the fire-lighted hogan. She watched Hobah's blue shadow moving along the wall. It made her think of Turquoise Woman on her way to the Western Waters.

"Uncle must tell us again of Turquoise Woman," she said to herself; "I will ask him to tell us when next he comes to my mother's hogan."

"Hogan, my hogan, my hogan blessed," sang the far rider.

Darkness came swiftly into the desert. Night came upon the People there.

The family moved their sheepskins out under the stars. One pelt alone was left inside, not used, not needed. It lay to one side, partly unrolled, wholly neglected. It was Big Brother's bed waiting for him to come home.

Outside, the night was clear and the stars hung low. Mother moved quietly, unrolling the sheepskins, tucking in the blankets. Doli lay upon her pelt in the soft, warm sand, in the warm, still night. Mother's hand found her hand in the darkness, softly, lightly, swiftly brushing it, like a raindrop, almost. Doli slept.

The next morning, after sunup, after breakfast, after Hobah had taken the flocks to graze, Uncle came riding around the red rocks and up through the sandwash. Uncle came riding, his arms held stiffly, elbows pointing outward, and jerking up and down with the pony's trotting. Doli stood by her mother's loom under the juniper tree, watching him coming. She stood still, waiting, feeling happy to see him. Uncle was young, almost as young as Big Brother. He was gay-acting and gay-looking. He

wore tight blue jeans and a bright red shirt and a big
black hat. His hair was long like Father's and he wore it
tied in a fat queue wrapped with long white cord.

Mother was beginning a new blanket. She was string-
ing her loom. She was letting Doli help her. Mother's yarn
that she had sheared from her sheep, had spun and dyed,
was rolled neatly into balls and was piled on the sheepskin beside them. Mother saw Uncle trotting his pony
through the sandwash. She smiled at Doli. She was pleased
to see her younger brother coming.

Father was making a silver ring. His workbench was a cottonwood stump. His tools were a hammer, a sandstone mold, and leather bellows. He sat cross-legged on the ground with his head bent low over his work, but he heard Uncle come riding around the red rocks.

Work stopped. They waited for Uncle.

Uncle lifted his pony into a run until they were just beyond the clearing of the juniper tree. Then Uncle made him stop with stiffened legs in a cloud of flying sand. It made Doli laugh to see Uncle's pony stop so quickly that it almost sat down.

Now that he had arrived in a dashing way, Uncle felt that he could take his time. So he sat there, looking at the waiting family. Then he got off slowly, throwing his pony's reins to the ground so it would not stray. He walked slowly to the shade of the hogan wall. He sat down slowly, saying not a word. His pony, reins dragging, began to graze on the sparse clumps of green.

Now all was stillness where but a time before was swift-moving action. Father came over to the hogan shade. He sat down by Uncle. He rolled himself a cigarette. He gave Uncle a little brown paper and his bag of tobacco and a match. He nodded to Uncle, meaning, "You may smoke." Uncle rolled a cigarette. He lit it, using the match that Father used and putting his own match carefully in the pocket of his bright red shirt. Now both men puffed their tobacco. Smoke came. Two blue lines curled upward.

Then Father spoke gravely to Uncle. "Greetings, Younger Brother," he said. Uncle answered gravely, "Greetings, Elder Brother."

Doli went near them. She stood shyly by her father, looking away from the loved Uncle whom she wanted so badly to see. "Greetings, Small One." Uncle spoke softly, looking straight ahead. He did not want to frighten the little Bluebird.

Doli, still not looking, put the bag of candy down

where Uncle could reach it. She said to her father, "It is a gift for him."

Uncle picked up the limp bag of squeezed and melted candy. He looked at his pony. He said, "I, too, have a gift to offer."

Uncle took from inside his shirt a small brown bundle. He handed it to Father. Mother left her weaving and came over to look at the brown paper package. Everyone looked at it. Then Father untied the string. Two deerskin moccasins with silver buttons on the sides stood proudly in the crumpled paper. Father took Doli in his arms and put the moccasins on her small brown feet. Doli looked at them. They were beautiful. She felt them. They were soft to the touch.

Presently Mother went to the well for water. She carried a large bucket. Her yellow-brown skirts swished softly as she walked through the sand. Doli went with her. Her yellow-brown skirts swished softly. She carried a little bucket. The loose sands slid into the tiny footprints the moccasins made.

Mother filled her pail with water at the well. Doli filled hers. Water splashed on her foot. She saw it, but she did not feel it. She pushed her foot out from the flounces of her skirts and poured more water on it. She watched the water flashing silver on its way down, but when it touched her foot she felt neither cold nor wetness.

Doli looked up at her mother. Her eyes were big with surprise. The moccasins were shelters. They were like little houses for her feet. They were good. They must like her small brown feet!

She and Mother walked back through the sand to the hogan. They went inside. The hogan was clean and cool and quiet. Sunlight came in at the doorway and lay like a bright blanket on the sand of the floor. Mutton cooked over the coals in a big black pot. The hogan cat washed its face and shook out its whiskers to dry. Far away came the tinkle of the bell goat with the flock that Hobah herded slowly to the waterhole. Doli looked up at her mother. They smiled together, a quick little understanding smile that said, "We are glad to be together in this hogan because it is beautiful and good."

III. THE FLOCK

"Come, Small One, the day is calling. Already your sister takes our flocks from the corral."

Doli opened her eyes to the world about her. Her mother sat before the out-of-doors fire making fried bread for the morning meal. The sheepskin beds of the rest of the family had been rolled away against the walls of the hogan. Breakfast preparations were on the floor. A blackened coffee pot, three tin cups, a bowl of sugar, and the stew pot made up the breakfast table. Outside the fat squares of yellow fried bread bobbed about in the kettle of boiling grease or were piled temptingly in a flat-bottomed basket.

Doli rubbed her eyes with small brown fists, put on the precious moccasins, and sat patiently waiting for Mother to comb her hair with the short end of the cornhusk broom. She ate breakfast slowly, although she was excited. She wanted to hurry. She wanted to be off with Hobah, walking along with the hurrying sheep. Never before had she been allowed to help herd the flock, for until now she had been her mother's helper. Her work had been around the hogan, the loom, and the cooking fire. But today she was to go with Hobah. She was beginning her sixth summer and it was time that she learned all the different kinds of woman's work.

She, like the other members of the family, had sheep and goats of her own and, while they were all herded together in one flock, everyone, even the little Doli, knew the sheep that belonged to each person. Mother owned most of the flock, but Father had sheep, Big Brother and Hobah and Doli had sheep. Whether they lived at home or not, whether they helped with the flock or not, their sheep and goats and lambs and kids were tended and cared for.

When Doli reached the door of the hogan, Hobah had crossed the drywash with the flock. Little Bluebird set out briskly to follow her. Mother gave Doli a can of stones to be used as a rattle to hurry the slow sheep. Then she stood aside, watching her daughters as they went out across the sun-drenched sand.

The goats hurried ahead, but the sheep made slower progress. Stupid creatures though they were, they yet seemed to know that haste would not make the scanty grass blades thicker nor the waterhole more cooling to thirsty throats.

Slowly, on and on, the flock moved forward. Every blade of green gave way before their steady hunger.

Sun-Carrier moved as the flock moved. Noon came. They gained the longed-for waterhole.

The sheep bunched together. Their sharp hoofs made bubbling mud of the sticky clay sides of the pool. Their woolly faces dipped deep into the stagnant wetness.

Doli and Hobah rested. There was little shade in the

sand-flat world fenced in by red rocks. But one cloud broke the blue above them.

Sun-Carrier looked down on the girls, the sheep, and the goats. They were the small living things in the big emptiness of sand. Heat rose in waves above the waterhole and sheep smell thickened the air. There was no wind, no breeze, no breath of air. The world was hot and still. It was so frighteningly big and so terribly still.

Doli looked around her. She thought of her mother in the shade of the home hogan. Perhaps her mother was weaving, making the blanket grow beneath her swift fingers. Perhaps the hogan cat was looking for Doli and wanting to play. Doli stretched. She felt hot and tired. It was better to be at home, she thought, but women had to tend the sheep. It was their work. She rattled the can her mother had given her, and an old goat came over and looked at her as if to say, "That's good. You must rattle the can at us as your mother does."

Hobah's voice cut through the hot noonday silence. She began telling the Small One of the Yei, the kind ones and the terrible ones who lived unseen somewhere about them. Hobah spoke softly and a little fearfully. Someone must tell these things to the small Bluebird child, but she hoped there were no listening Yei near by to hear her lest she displease them some way. It was well to have care when one talked of Holy Things.

A lazy lizard rested by Hobah's hand. Hobah stopped talking for fear the lizard was a messenger of the Yei. Who knows, she thought, what lizards really are!

Above them the little lone cloud yawned and stretched itself in two.

Doli thought it better to talk of safer things than Yei. "Why are White Men?" she wanted to know, but Hobah could not answer. "We are the People and these White Men are strangers," she said. "Perhaps our uncle can answer us that. We will let him tell us. He has more years of wisdom, our uncle."

The lizard wiggled away. The girls were careful not to look where it was going. A messenger of the gods would not like little girls to possess Yei secrets.

Far away among the red rocks some Navajo boy was singing to his flock. "Listen, Small One," Hobah whispered. His words came to them like flying birds swooping low over the sands.

"My ewe sheep

That live on flowers,"

he sang,

"That live on pollen,

That live on dewdrops,"

he sang,

"They are spreading around me.

I walk among them.

All is well.

All is good."

Time moved slowly. Noon made way for afternoon. The sheep drowsed, heads turned inward close against one another.

"Why did Big Brother have anger when he came to see us?" Doli whispered the words. She was afraid to ask them, but she must know.

"Hush, you, speak not about him or our father will be angry, because our mother's son has given up the ways of the People and lives now as a White Man. He comes no more to our mother's hogan."

Doli dug her small feet deep in the hot sands. Again she felt the sickness of longing come to her. Her heart hit against her velvet blouse and a hot pain beat in her

slender throat. She sat there, hugging her knees and looking far out to that place where the above-world stooped
down to touch the yellow sands of this middle-world.

"Is it the distant School land, Elder Sister, that took
him from us? Will it reach its strong hand out for you?"

Then a strange thing happened. A look of wanting
came to Hobah's eyes, an excited, eager look of waiting.
"School is good, I think," she said. "When I go I will
learn the new things to help make the old things better.
Always will I be a daughter of the People, but I want to
have much wisdom, knowing many ways. There is good,
some good, in all things, I think." Pride lived in the deep
dark eyes of Elder Sister. Doli saw and understood.
Hobah's mind would seek new knowledge, but her feet
would stay firmly in the footprints of her mother's
trail.

Little Bluebird got up and went among the sheep. Here
were her sheep, her mother's and father's sheep, her sister's and brother's. There would always be sheep as long
as there were children of the People to tend them. She
knew them, these woolly creatures; they had to be cared
for, to give life in return. She did not know these things
with words. She was too little, but she knew them in her

heart. She knew in her heart that some day the flock would be her work and her comfort. There would always be need for someone to stay at home where things were not strange. There would always be need for some daughter to stay at home to tend the sheep and the babies and the fire.

Heat time of day passed. Sun-Carrier moved a little faster now that he neared the western sky where Turquoise Woman awaited him. The children started the flock on the home trail. Hobah walked among the flock, shaking her can rattle at the stragglers. Doli lagged behind. She watched her elder sister, so slender, so straight, so sure in all things that were a part of her. Evening shadows went with her like a blanket of blue mist. "She is Turquoise Woman, my sister, I think," said the small one trudging through the sand.

A tiny gray field mouse scampered into the bushes. A dove sorrowfully sang his sunset song. Blue smoke from the hogan supper fire made a straight line upward, like a greeting telling them, "Home is here."

The sheep crowded together, bleating and pushing. The goats strayed and had to be scolded. Hobah took down the bars of the night corral and the woolly animals crowded in, glad for rest and glad for the coolness of night.

Mother was standing at the hogan door. She smiled at her daughters, but she had a special smile for the little Bluebird who this day had begun woman's work.

Uncle was at the hogan. He had come for a night's visit. Father had made a piñon fire not far from the juniper tree, and after evening food had been cleared away the family sat around the smoldering coals. Far into the night Father and Uncle sang. Some of the songs were sound music without words. The one Doli liked best went:

"Ya he ya ho
Ya he ya ho
Yo hay O
Ya na."

The men sang and Doli dozed close to her mother, her heart filled with well-being.

As she dozed she half dreamed of Turquoise Woman, the beautiful Navajo girl of long ago whom Sun had wanted for his wife. The People had not wanted her to go, but after a time she listened to Sun and journeyed far off to the Western Waters where Sun had built her a hogan of coral- and turquoise-colored clouds and rainbows.

Next winter when the hogan was bright with fire and the family sat close and warm together, Doli would ask again and again for Uncle to tell her the story of Turquoise Woman. Now she awakened suddenly, for Father was singing alone. He was singing softly, and as he sang it seemed to Doli that he looked with sadness at his eldest daughter. Father sang:

"Turquoise Woman going
   To western far places,
   To the Western World,
   To the Western Waters,
   Turquoise Woman thither going,
   Thither going,
   Going, going."

"Turquoise Woman, my sister," murmured Doli sleepily. "Beautiful my sister, stay here with us. Do not go away."

Mother unrolled the sheepskins and the blankets. She placed her daughters' beds beside hers under the juniper shelter. She smoothed their blankets. She smiled good night to them and Doli knew, although no one said the words, that Mother was thinking of the time when Hobah must go off to School. Hobah was twelve now, she had finished the books the Day School taught. She was the same age Big Brother had been when he had gone to the distant Boarding School.

Mother sat looking into the firelight, wondering about the two trails, the Red Man's and the White Man's, that met and crossed. Could they not be made to go on side by side?

Father and Uncle talked and were silent and talked again. Mother sat silent under the stars, looking inward.

Hobah slept; sure in all things, untroubled, she slept. Doli was tired. The day had been hard. She was sleepy, but she was happy too, for this day she had started the work that would keep her always close to the hogan. She had herded her sheep.

IV. NIGHT CAMP

Summer passed slowly with long hot days and warm clear nights. Doli went with Hobah to take the sheep to the waterhole and back again at sunset to the night corral. August came, dressed in yellow sunlight.

The young wife of Uncle journeyed over from To-hatchi district to care for the flock so that Mother, Hobah, and Doli could go to Canyon de Chelly to gather in their share of the summer's crop of peaches. Uncle's young wife had been to Boarding School. She could speak English words with much swiftness and was said to have much knowledge.

Doli was shy and refused to eat or speak the evening of her arrival. She watched Hobah guardedly as she served her mother's guest with food. Her sister, Doli thought, had great beauty in her quiet way of moving. Doli wondered if Uncle's wife liked the way in which Hobah moved about the hogan. She wondered if Uncle's wife would tend their sheep properly and hoped the sheep would not like her. She was glad that Hobah had few words with this young Navajo woman who knew so well the ways of the School world.

Always there was fear that School would stretch out its strong hand for Hobah, and always there was knowledge that when the hand of the School world beckoned, Hobah would go.

Uncle's young wife refused to sleep on the family's collection of sheepskins. Instead, she made her bed of many store blankets which Uncle brought in from under the seat of his wagon. Before she slept, she laid away her ornaments of silver and turquoise and coral, her rings and bracelets, her moccasins and velvet blouse, her three wide ruffled calico skirts. She put on something else before she slept.

Long into the night, Doli felt the wakeful body of her sister lying beside her and her heart knew why Hobah was not sleeping. Doli's unconquered heart knew and resented and defied.

At last she slept, fitfully, restlessly, dreaming, and it seemed but a minute until her mother called her, telling her it was time to get up. The world about the hogan looked unreal and unfriendly, filled with the cold light of before dawn, but no one had time to comfort the little Bluebird. There was work to be done.

Sunup time found the three women-people in the back of Father's wagon. Father was driving and singing to his horses. His strong, high voice rolled on before them:

"Hither go we to the far country,
  Hither go my horses to the mountains.
  Blessed are my horses.
  They are good, my blessed horses.
  Hither go my horses to the mountains.
  Hither go we to the mountains."

Uncle came riding behind them. He was sitting his pony without a saddle and with only a rope around the pony's nose. Uncle was not going to gather peaches. He had wanted to go, but his young wife had told him, "No." So Uncle was riding behind, but only as far as night camp. Early tomorrow he would be back with his wife again.

Doli was hungry. She had not eaten. A hunger pain sat in her stomach. She tried leaning forward to chase it away. She shut her eyes to it, trying to hide it from herself. It stayed. It would not go away. It was hunger. It wanted food. It seemed to say, "Last night and this morning you ate nothing. Food has not been in you since Uncle's wife entered your mother's hogan."

Doli looked at her mother. "It is long since we have eaten, my Mother," she said. Mother was not kind. She would not look at her hungry little girl. She answered only, "Food was placed before you, Little One. Bad thoughts are as rocks in the stomach."

Doli looked at Hobah, but her elder sister's eyes were not for her. They were on the far places. They did not see a hungry little girl.

Doli pulled her blanket high around her head. She sat without moving, looking at nothing.

The wagon went bumping along the road with Father's horses going steadily in front and Uncle's pony trotting behind. Sometimes they met other wagons. Once a truck passed them, but Father did not seem frightened. He kept driving his horses along.

In mid-afternoon the air became thick with sand. All around the skyline were giant whirlwinds. Uncle said maybe they were returned warriors of an enemy people. Uncle said he did not like whirlwinds. One did not know what made them dance and turn and whirl.

Father stopped singing. Mother pulled her store blanket about her shoulders and wrapped her daughters within its folds.

The sky darkened. Sun-Carrier hid his face. Sand blew in choking clouds. It was hard to see and harder to breathe. Flying sand stung their faces and wind beat their bodies. Father turned the horses about and they stood with lowered heads while the wind tossed the world up and threw it down again in anger.

Doli felt guilty. She felt that the storm had been sent as punishment for her. She had thought badly of Uncle's wife. She had hoped the sheep would not like her and would give her trouble. "Perhaps she is an evil woman," she told herself, "and can bring punishment to me because I think bad thoughts about her." She wished she dared tell Uncle about his evil wife who had caused her, his favorite child, to be punished by the sand storm. She peeped out from her blanket at the sand-filled world. Uncle sat his pony with bowed head, letting the sand beat against his back. Mother and Hobah had their faces covered. Father on the wagon seat sat hunched against the wind. No one looked comfortable. Everyone was suffering from the sand storm. Doli thought perhaps it would be better not to tell them who had caused this. "When we return home to my mother's hogan and all the sheep are lost and maybe stolen, then I can tell them about that woman," she promised herself, ducking her head back within the folds of her mother's blanket.

After a time the sands quieted and lay still upon the ground. The wind went off to some other place and left the air dusty, sand-smelling, but still. The wagon jogged along the road again and Uncle laughed and made his pony run. He was always gay.

At sunset time night camp was made. Doli was glad to get out of the wagon and stretch her stiffened body. She was glad to run around helping her mother cook food. She was glad to eat it, too, sand-filled though it was. She ate her share and a part of Hobah's.

Other Navajos were camped about, and by the time the stars came out their campfires were dotting the sandy hills. The smells of coffee, smoke, and cooking meats and breads blotted out the smell of sand dust. Laughter was heard, and bits of talk and snatches of song. Dogs fought and snarled and growled and barked at other dogs and at the moon. Horses moved restlessly, their hobbled feet thudding the ground.

Father and Uncle were to sleep under the wagon, but they went away somewhere to play some games with other men. Mother did not like it. She kept sitting up from her blankets in the wagon bed beside her daughters. She kept looking at the campfire yonder where Father and Uncle were playing the game with the other men.

Stars winked at the campfires and the people laughed and sang. It was good to be one of the People. It was good to be going with the family to Canyon de Chelly for peaches. Doli stretched out beneath her blanket covers. She did not have bad thoughts about anyone now, nor hunger, nor fear that Hobah would go away. She had only deep happiness to be here at night camp on the way to the orchards of Canyon de Chelly.

V. GATHERING PEACHES

Doli was up long before sunrise time of morning. Mother was cross about something and scolded and grumbled to herself as she dragged the family cooking pots from the fire by the wagon.

Uncle had not gone home last night as he should have gone. He had stayed playing games with the men. Now he had gone, riding into the gray of coming day. He had to hurry back to his young wife. She would not be pleased because he was late. Mother was not pleased either. She had turned her back on Uncle while Hobah put the morning food before him. Uncle had pretended not to notice. He had laughed and acted gay, but now he was running his pony. He was in a hurry. He and his running pony quickly were lost to sight in the soft-misted morning.

Doli went to find her father. He was at the far end of the circle of wagons and by the light of a breakfast fire was playing a game with an old Navajo man. Old men and young men and a few boys sat watching them.

Father balanced a flat stick on a smooth stone. He put pennies in a row on the flat stick. Then Father said in the English, "Heads," and he flipped the stick. The watchers, sitting on their heels, moved in nearer so they could see which pennies were "Heads" and which were "Tails." Father and the old man picked up the pennies they had won. Then it was the old man's turn to line the pennies on the stick and flip them. Father had a little pile of money on the sand between his knees. He seemed well pleased. All the watching men joked with him and with the old man. They said, "Perhaps your money has eyes in the 'Head' so it can see which way to fall." They said, "Perhaps you will go to Gallup with all this money and ride the train." They joked the old man, too. They told him he was too old. His money could not see.

One by one the onlookers left. Wagons started away on the day's journey. Presently Father pocketed his pennies and he and Doli went to Mother's cooking fire. But the fire had been put out with sand, the breakfast food, the pots and pans had been stored away. The horses were hitched and Mother sat well within her blanket in the back of the wagon. Doli did not venture near her. She took her place with Hobah at the other end of the wagon bed. Father looked at Mother, but he did not speak. He got up on the wagon seat. He took the reins. He looked around at night camp, then he spoke to his horses and the wagon lurched over the sand humps to the road.

Hobah's eyes were shining. She was very happy. She bent her dark head close to her sister's and whispered excitedly to her. On an ant hill not from from the cook fire she had found a precious thing. "I think it is a gift from the Yei. It is a good sign, a good omen, I think," she whispered. She opened her hand that Doli might see the possession. There in her slender brown palm lay a perfect garnet. It burned deep red in the early sunlight. "I have heard that travelers find these stones in our desert country," she told her sister, "but that I should find one is a good sign for me, I think."

Doli was impressed. "It might be a gift from Sun-Carrier. He might want you," she said.

Hobah laughed, "No, of course not that, but a sign of something to come that is good."

Up front, Father on the wagon seat began to sing, but Mother told him to be still. "We are not taking crows to gather peaches," she told him. Father made the horses go faster, but he, himself, sat quietly. Doli wondered if he had eaten breakfast. She thought not and if that were true she knew why Father had wanted to sing. It was to chase the hunger pain away. Poor Father! Doli wondered how long Mother would continue to be cross about something.

The family did not make camp at noon. Mother told Hobah to give out pieces of cold fried bread to be eaten instead of lunch.

In the late afternoon the family arrived at Canyon de Chelly. Hobah knew about the place. She had come with her grandmother many times before. Now she told the things she knew to the little girl beside her.

Canyon de Chelly is the loved place of the Navajos.

It is here that the Home God lives. It is here that the ancient peach trees grow in stunted dwarfed shapes, bearing small sweet peaches. It is here that the People come, year after year, with the children, the babies, and the old ones. If a mother owns peach trees in Canyon de Chelly, she leaves them to her daughters that her daughters' daughters may own them in the years to come. Hobah had two peach trees that her grandmother had given her, and Doli hoped that she, herself, would soon own a tree. Grandmother had many trees and if she came this year, and Doli was a good girl, perhaps, perhaps . . . Doli put her hand over her mouth as she always did when she was pleased. It would be good to own a peach tree.

Doli slid out of the wagon almost before Father had it stopped. They had stopped in a patch of green near Spider Rock. This would be camp for several days. Giant rocks of sunset colors rose up from the damp sand bottom of the canyon to meet the blue of the world above the canyon walls. Cliffs of colored rocks closed them in. A strange hush filled this Holy Place. High up in the heart of the cliff wall above the canyon in a cave there had been built a white pueblo house, shining like pure white shell in the rose-colored rock.

Doli turned her eyes from such beauty. It might not be well to see too much of wonder. The Yei might not be pleased that such a small girl saw the magic of such great beauty.

She looked instead at Father, standing by his wagon. He was counting his pennies. Mother's back was turned to him, but Doli knew that Mother knew what Father was doing. Father squatted in the sand. He made two piles of pennies, one very little and the other one big. Then Father looked at Mother's back. He made the small pile big. Then he looked at it some more and penny by penny he made it bigger, until at last it was the big pile and the other one had just a few. Father looked at Mother again. She still had her back turned toward him. He put the few pennies in his pocket. He scooped the big pile up in his hand. He spoke softly to Mother. "You might like these, I think," he said. "Last night and this morning I won them playing a game with an old man, but I almost forgot to give them to you." Mother turned around. She took the money. She looked at it closely and then she smiled at Father.

Doli smiled too, and Hobah smiled. Mother was not cross now. Everything was right again.

Father unhitched his horses. He took them to the spring for water. He went far down the canyon and as he went he sang. Other voices joined his singing, growing in rounded sounds, high and piercingly sweet:

"Since the ancient days, I have planted it.
  Since the time of first-coming, I have planted it,
  The corn, the great corn plant.
  It will eat the dew of the dark cloud.
  It will eat the mist of the dark cloud.
  It is tied to the ground with rainbows.
  It is tied to the ground with sunbeams,
  The corn, the great corn plant."

Many voices now were singing and the canyon walls echoed the song in muffled sounds like drum beats.

Doli smelled the smoke of her mother's supper fire. She saw Hobah returning from a neighboring camp, carrying peaches for their evening meal. Doli felt happy. She felt clean and strong. She went to walk beside her mother from the wagon to the spring to the cooking fire. She put her small hand in her mother's strong one. "Always will I come to gather peaches with you, my Mother," she whispered. "Always will I stay with you."

Her mother looked down at her. Her strong hand tightened lovingly about the small one. She answered, "Always you will meet the things that come to you, Little Last One. Always you will walk the Beautiful Trail wherever it leads you. Remember."

Father came back with the horses. He was eating peaches. He teased Mother a little and joked and laughed with those who passed by. He was pleased that Mother was happy again. He said to himself, "What is money! In a day or two, perhaps, I can win some more." He unrolled his blanket early after supper and only laughed good-naturedly when Mother said, "Tonight the night bird sleeps, I see."

The next day everyone was busy gathering peaches, eating peaches, drying peaches for winter use, and packing some in the wagon to have when they got home and to trade with those who did not have peach trees in the old, old orchard at Canyon de Chelly.

Everyone helped everyone else at times. Mother and Hobah and Doli helped Grandmother, who had come with Mother's oldest sister and her three small boys. Just as Doli had thought, Grandmother gave her a peach tree. It was a little tree not much larger than the little girl and it

bent over like an old man offering the Bluebird child its fruits.

In as many days as Doli had fingers on one small hand, the family went home again from the canyon. Everyone was happy. The peach crop had been a good one. In the back of the wagon there were peaches for winter, for Uncle and his wife, and peaches to sell to the Trader. Father and Mother and Hobah sat on the wagon seat and Doli stood between her Father's knees. She was helping him drive the horses. Under the seat in a flour sack were Doli's peaches from Doli's tree.

It had been good to go to Canyon de Chelly, but now it was good to be home again. The flock had been well cared for. Not a sheep was missing. The flock looked happy, the sheep and the goats and the half-grown lambs and kids. Doli was surprised, but she felt pleased about it. Perhaps Uncle's wife was not an evil woman after all. Hobah seemed to like her. Mother liked her. When Doli gave Uncle his share of the peaches from her tree, she shyly put a pile of the sweet little fruit beside her uncle's wife.

Life was the same as it had been before they went away. Hobah and Doli spent the days with the sheep and the nights under the stars by the juniper tree or in the shelter of the fire-lighted hogan.

The days were long and warm. Mother wove busily, or spun new yarn and dyed it, butchered a lamb, ground cornmeal when it was needed, and cooked for her family. Father rode his horses, went to the Trading Post, or hammered and fashioned his dreams into silver ornaments. Uncle came over to visit, sometimes alone, sometimes with his young wife, with relatives, with friends.

Summer passed. All was well.

VI. THE SING

Hobah, Mother, and Doli sat near the hogan door waiting for Father to come back from the Trading Post. Hobah was turning her garnet in the evening light. She seemed pleased with its flashings. Mother was just sitting, but now and then she looked anxiously at her elder daughter.

64

Doli was restless. She wished that Uncle were coming for a visit. How nice it would be, she thought, if Father and Uncle would ride into the firelight, bringing Big Brother with them. She pictured them as they would look on their horses, singing, maybe, riding up to the hogan out of the shadows of evening.

Mother began to sing and after a little Hobah joined in the soft chanting:

"Ana yi a ana yi
  Ana yi e ya he ya
  Yo."

Sounds of ponies' hoof beats came to them dimly from around the red rock across the sandwash. The singing stopped. Father came riding. Uncle came riding. The women folk watched them come.

The men reined their ponies before the hogan door and dismounted. Father went into the hogan. Mother and the girls went into the hogan. Uncle stayed outside to tend the ponies.

Father stood near the firepit. He had anger in him. It made his still face gray. Doli shivered. She knew fear, but Mother and Hobah waited quietly. Father's anger broke. It showered the hogan with glinting cold.

He spoke. "White Man at the Trading Post tells me that in two weeks' time they will come after yonder girl to go to the Boarding School. He has paper showing that she must go. Your first-born went when paper said to take him. He went to School to gather in of wisdom. Does he come now to your fire to share his learning with us? No, he comes not here. He scorns the ways of the People. He leaves empty the heart of her who bore him."

Father was silent. He looked stern and sad. He looked at Hobah and then at Mother. "I can take this girl to Doke-oslid where no White hand can reach her. Speak you. What do you want? What is it to be?"

Hobah went quietly to her mother's side. She stood there, slender and tall and proud, waiting for her mother's words. If her mother let her go to that place where one gathered in of learning, she would go gladly.

Her mother's words came. They came slowly as if from the deep well of her heart. They came steadily. They did not falter. She had thought it all out in many hours of many nights' wakefulness. She knew what it was she had to say.

"Life called my first-born," she told Father. "I gave him. That he returns not to my side is reason for grief,

not anger. I have placed this girl's feet on the straight road. If her trail circles back to my fire, it is well. If it takes her into unknown places, my heart will still sing because she will go unafraid. When the School man comes this girl will go to School."

Father went out of the hogan. He and his pony went off into the night. Mother and Hobah prepared food. They served Uncle where he sat smoking by the juniper tree. They ate and cleared away the supper things. Hobah raked the fire coals and unrolled the family beds.

Doli sat in the doorway, her feet drawn under her, her small hands tightly folded. She had no thoughts. Her heart was filled with darkness like the night world.

Outside, Uncle smoked and looked at the stars. Mother and Hobah prepared themselves for bed. They were like that, those two. Their hearts might ache or they might be overjoyed, but they did not give way. They quietly did the work that was to be done, as if tending the body needs might help keep the feet steady on the trail beneath them.

Night unfolded slowly. Night winds blew cool across the desert. Night voices broke the stillness as wild things called their mates.

Doli sat hunched in the doorway. Her small, tired head drooped over her small, clenched hands. She did not feel the night winds nor hear the night voices. Hobah was going. Hobah was leaving the friendly shelter of Mother's hogan. Her eyes were dry, but her mouth tasted of tears. Hobah was going to the School as Big Brother had gone. Hobah was going out into the world beyond the red rocks and the sandwash. What would she do without her? What would the sheep do? How would they get along? How could they go day after day, the sheep and the small Blue-bird girl, alone to the waterhole and back alone to the night corral?

Uncle threw away his cigarette. It made a lighted trail through the darkness. Hobah got up from her sheepskin. She came over to the little girl. She smoothed her hair. She took off the small brown moccasins with their gay silver buttons. Her hands felt sure and strong. They felt cool against Doli's hot little face. Hobah helped her to her sheepskin, she spread her blanket around Doli. She sat beside her. Somewhere the moon came up and filled the hogan with gray light. Somewhere a coyote barked, a lonesome sound. Outside the hogan, Uncle unrolled his blanket and went to bed under the stars. Hobah drew

the blanket across the hogan doorway. She came back to sit beside her sister's sheepskin until finally sleep came to close the tired eyes of the little Bluebird.

Miles away, Father rode steadily. He rode with a purpose. His goal was the hogan of Dawn Singer, Navajo Medicine Man. If his daughter must go within the White Man's world, let her go prepared! Never again would a child of his go forth alone into that strange country. Hobah would take with her Holy Medicine whose power would keep her untouched by strange ways so that, School ended, she would return to him. He would have a Holy Sing for this precious child of his. Dawn Singer would come, although his price was high. Father did not care how many sheep he had to pay. He did not care how many baskets, how much flour and cornmeal the Sing would cost him. Father knew that his wife would agree with him; he knew it, for her heart was sick although she clothed it well with words.

Father trotted his pony steadily into the dawn.

Late the next night, when he returned to his family, Mother accepted quietly the news of the Sing. Yes, Father could have what sheep were needed. Yes, she had gladness that Hobah would go forth well clothed in the garments of Holy Song.

At once, life within the home circle quickened. Mother went to the Trading Post and came back with yards of bright calico, bright velvets, bright braids and bindings and thread. Uncle's wife came over to stay until after the Sing. She took the calico and velvet and braid and thread and went over to the Day School to use the sewing machine. She went day after day until she had made everyone a new blouse and three wide, ruffled skirts, gathered and braided and bound. Uncle's wife knew how to do so many things and do them well. Doli wondered if Hobah would learn to sew on a sewing machine.

The heavy grinding stones were put by the hogan door. Word of the Sing had traveled swiftly. All the relatives came to help. Corn was ground. Goats and sheep were butchered, roasted, and boiled.

Dawn Singer was to give the Moving-Upward Chant, that Holy Song of one night's lasting which never failed to guard against all evil.

Everyone worked all day and at night the women rested and the men sang and talked.

Full days went by in quick succession.

Day before the night of the Sing dawned in yellow and red, a good omen.

Dawn Singer began his sand painting for the Sing. On a clean bed of yellow sand he made five rainbow goddesses for the five rainbow colors. From his partly closed hand he sifted the colored sands to draw his figures straight and true. The goddesses were slender and strong-looking. They wore rainbow garters.

To the east, he made white lines of white sands and there he placed a feathered prayer stick of mountain mahogany. To the south, he made blue lines with blue sands and there he placed a feathered prayer stick of coyote-corn. To the west, he made yellow lines with

yellow sands and there he planted a feathered prayer stick made of juniper. To the north, he made black lines with black sands and there he put a feathered prayer stick of cherry wood.

Everywhere he put pieces of white string as the sign of a straight life trail.

Dawn Singer was famous for good medicine among his people. Now Navajos for miles and miles away came in wagons, on horseback, and in a few trucks to the Sing of the Moving-Upward Chant. They came to be present at the Holy Time. They came to walk the Holy Trail. They came that good might go back with them.

Doli felt the holiness of the chanting, the prayers, the ceremony, and the thoughts of the People. Her heart was cleansed of its pain, at least for a little while.

As the long shadows of late afternoon promised sun-set, Hobah was brought from the hogan. Her new calico skirts were stiff and full about her. Her face shone with deep and happy feeling. She was serene. Life held wisdom close to her reaching. She was not afraid.

She was blessed with pollen, life-power of the sacred corn. The feathered prayer sticks and the sand painting were blessed with pollen.

Hobah was placed on the heart of the painting. As Dawn Singer chanted the Holy Song, Sun-Carrier put the sun away and the Holy Chant was finished. The many-colored sands were scattered to the four directions and up and down.

The visitors crowded around the hogan and the hogan clearing. After a time, when food was prepared, they ate heartily of the feast set before them. Then they sat, waiting for the new day while the men-singers blessed the night with Holy Song.

Morning dawned, ending the Sing. The Sun-Carrier, lifting the sun up out of the world of darkness in the eastern sky, looked down upon the Navajos, blessing them with light, with warmth, and with the promise of day.

VII.
HOBAH GOES TO SCHOOL

Only Hobah was awake to greet the morning. She looked over at her sister's sheepskin. It was empty. Hobah moved quietly from the hogan to find the little Bluebird. She looked in the shade of the juniper tree. Doli was not there. She was not by Mother's loom or Father's forge. At last Hobah found her, lying asleep under the wagon, her tired head pillowed against the comforting warmth of Yellow-Boy, the sheep dog. Hobah looked down at her little sister; her small brown face was tear-streaked, her mouth quivered even as she slept. Hobah touched gently the small one's shoulder. She called the little Blue-bird to wakefulness and beckoned her to follow.

Doli stumbled sleepily after her sister. The night's grieving had numbed her heart as the night's cold had numbed her body. She remembered that on this day Hobah was to leave her, but it meant little now against her crying need for sleep.

When the girls had reached the clearing by the sheep corral, Hobah spread her blanket for Doli to sit upon. They sat quietly, watching the sunrise. Doli leaned against her sister. The freshness of the morning was clearing her tired brain for thought.

At last Hobah spoke, "Little Bluebird, my younger Sister, do not grieve that today I leave you. I am of the People. Always will I return to the People. Look, my Sister! I give you this to keep for me until I return. It is my most precious possession. Take it." She handed Doli her garnet stone, gift from the Yei.

Doli looked at the garnet, burning blood-red in the

early sunlight. It was like a living thing. It was a living thing, a living promise that Elder Sister would come back again. The girls said nothing more. There was no need for words. Sun-Carrier rose in the blue above, calling the People to waken and meet the day.

Smoke from Mother's breakfast fire called the girls to food. They walked back to the hogan, Doli comforted by Hobah's promise, Hobah strengthened by it.

Breakfast was a silent meal. Each member of the family was busy with food and busy with his own thoughts.

After the family had eaten, Hobah put the breakfast things away. The hogan cat brushed against her skirts. Sunlight shone on her blue-black hair. Father went out to hitch his horses to the wagon. Mother busied herself putting bread and jerked meat and dried peaches in a flour sack for Hobah to take with her to the strange School place. No telling what kind of food she might have to eat when she got there, she thought.

Doli was wide awake now. She watched Hobah's every move. She watched her stoop down to pat the hogan cat. She watched her sweep the hogan floor. Then Mother called her elder daughter. She brushed her hair and tied and bound it with new yarn. A great cry of longing swelled the little sister's throat, but no cry escaped her tightly closed mouth. Hobah was ready.

A new calico skirt was put on over the ones that had been made for the Sing. Mother put her own best necklace of coral and turquoise over the proud head of her elder girl. The necklace was very old and had great value. It had belonged, years ago, to Grandmother's Mother. Mother gave Hobah a new store blanket.

The blanket covering the hogan door was pushed aside and Uncle and his young wife came in. They brought presents for Hobah. Uncle brought a sheepskin and a turquoise ring. Uncle's wife was shy with her gift. It was a small box-shaped package wrapped in flour sacking. Hobah opened it in breathless silence. Doli and Mother pushed close to get the first glimpse. Uncle pushed in, too. He knew what it was. He had seen it before, but not enough. He wanted to see it again. Uncle's wife stood aside, her eyes half closed, her hand over her mouth. Uncle's wife was pleased and excited, although she did not want to show it. She hoped Hobah would like the gift. She herself liked it very much.

Hobah unwrapped the flour sacking. She held a leather box in her hands. It was brown leather. It was fastened

queerly. Uncle said, "That way to fasten it is called a zipper." Uncle took the leather box. He pulled the zipper to open it. He pulled the zipper to close it. He showed Hobah how to pull the zipper, but he did not let her pull it. He pulled it himself. Inside there was a looking glass with a handle. There were a store brush and comb for the hair and a store brush for the teeth. They were a blue color, almost like turquoise. They were beautiful. Everyone looked at them and touched them. Even Uncle's wife looked at them again. Father came in. He looked too. Uncle showed him how the zipper fastener worked. Father liked that the best. He took the box from Uncle. He zipped it and unzipped it.

Finally, Father gave Hobah the leather zipper box. He went to get his gift for her. He brought it in. It was a fine new tin trunk. He had bought it at the Trading Post. Mother put the things that belonged to Hobah in her trunk. Doli had a gift for Hobah, too. She brought it into the crowded room, her pet lamb now almost grown. Everyone laughed but Hobah. She said she liked that gift the best of all. She said for Doli to keep it for her. She would add it to her flock when she came back from School.

There was a call from outside. Uncle went to see who made it. It was Grandmother and Mother's oldest sister and her three sons and her husband. They had come with gifts for Hobah and to tell her good-by. Father and Uncle went outside with Mother's oldest sister's husband. Grandmother could then come into the hogan.

There was much talking by everyone. The morning grew into almost noon. At last Father sent Uncle in to say that Hobah should go. The man with the School bus had said he would be at the Trading Post early in the morning. He had said for the fathers to bring their children early in the morning so as not to keep him waiting.

Uncle said, "It is now almost noon so perhaps the girl and her father should be starting. The man with the School bus will be impatient, I think." Mother said yes, it was time to go. She stood before Hobah. She placed her two hands on Hobah's straight young shoulders. She looked briefly into her daughter's eyes. Then she turned away. This was a day of many duties. It called for work and not for grieving. She had done all she could do for this girl child. Mother turned away; work called her.

Father was waiting in the wagon; he held out his hand to help his daughter climb onto the high seat. Then he picked up the reins and turned his horses into the road that led through the sandwash and out into the world beyond the red rocks.

Hobah was going. The White hand had reached out for her.

"My Sister, oh, my Sister, my Sister," cried the little Doli standing alone by the juniper tree. "My Sister. My Sister."

The world stood still. The things of the world were silent for the moment that Father's wagon carrying Hobah went around the red rocks to that which lay beyond.

Hobah was gone. She was gone. They had taken her. Doli remembered Big Brother's going, only he had gone singing through the sandwash that first time that he had gone away. He had gone singing, raising his hand in laughing farewell. Hobah sat silent. She sat beside Father, her blanket pulled high around her. She sat stiff and straight, not looking backward.

Now she was gone. Even the noise of the wagon wheels had been blotted out by distance. She was gone. The world stood still.

Doli did not cry. She had no tears. But her eyes were blinded by pain as she stumbled back to the night corral to take the goats and the sheep to graze.

They were glad to be freed. It was long past time. Now they crowded about her. Their bodies, pushing against her, felt good. Sheep smell was around her. It was comforting. It was something known.

The little girl and the flock went through the sandwash. The sharp pointed hoofs of the animals quickly marked out the tracks of Father's wagon.

Doli walked among the flock as Hobah had always done. A small proud feeling grew within her. She alone was tending the sheep. She alone was responsible for them.

The long day came to its close. No voice broke its stillness. The Sun-Carrier moved and the flock moved. The sheep ate their way to the waterhole and drank. Then slowly and steadily they ate their way back again to the night corral.

Uncle was waiting for Doli's return. He had brought over some corn which he said his wife had sent. He said she knew that Doli would be hungry after her day of herding. Grandmother had stayed for a visit. She wanted to help ease the hurt that Hobah's going had brought to Mother and to Doli. Father would be gone for several days. After he left Hobah at the Trading Post, he would go on to a Meeting. Grandmother would stay until Father returned.

Food tasted good after the day's work. Doli was tired. Sleep came to her almost before she could unroll her sheepskin bed beside the hogan fire.

VIII. AUTUMN

Autumn came to the red rock country. Fall winds blew across the sands. Nights grew longer and cooler. Days grew shorter and cooler.

Father brought in his garden crops, mostly corn and beans. Mother dried them and put them away in the dugout storeroom. She butchered a kid and cut and dried the meat into jerky. Father took the spring lambs to the Trading Post to sell to the Trader.

Autumn days passed as summer days had passed, slowly, one by one, weaving their design through the pattern of time.

Then came a day that began badly. Breakfast consisted only of goat milk and goat cheese. Mother had neglected her weaving during the time of the Sing, getting ready for it, getting Hobah ready for School, and getting the family food ready for winter. Now she must make up for the time that had been lost. Her blanket was not finished and she was out of red yarn.

Mother was cross. She was worried for fear she could not dye new yarn to match the other. She felt hurried. This morning she meant to card more wool, spin it, and dye it to match the other yarn. She had no time to cook for her family.

Doli felt cross, too. She felt hungry. She felt tired of the sheep. Today she would have liked to stay at home with her mother. She would have liked to watch her mother card the matted bits of gray wool into fluffy clouds of white. She would have liked to watch the flashing spindle turning under her mother's swift fingers.

She would have liked to help dye the yarn to a matching redness.

Instead, she must herd the sheep. She walked out slowly to the night corral. The sheep were impatient to be out. They pushed her roughly when she let down the bars.

The day went on as it had begun. A black kid strayed away from the flock. Doli sang to it as Uncle had taught her. She sang and sang, but the naughty young goat paid no attention to the song. Doli took out the Yei garnet from a little buckskin bag which she wore about her neck. She tried flashing it to bring the black kid back. Nothing happened. At last Doli put the garnet on a sand hump to guard the flock, while she herself went after the wanderer. The kid would not be driven. She had to half carry, half push it back. Twice the little girl and the young goat became tangled in wide, long skirts and went down together in the sand.

After a time the black kid was where he belonged again, but then Doli could not find the precious garnet. The Sun-Carrier had moved quite a way across the blue before the Yei stone was found on the sand hump just where it had been placed.

Doli was hot and dusty, hungry and tired. The sheep

were stupid and slow. All around the skyline rain showers could be seen, but none came to cool the hot air around the waterhole or to make the wind lie down. The sheep moved lazily. Neither singing nor rattling the stone-filled can could hurry them.

Afternoon dragged by. At dusk, far to the east, the little girl saw a rainbow. It was a beautiful rainbow arching across the sky with all its colors clear. Doli was glad that she knew she should not point at it. She remembered that Hobah had told her never to point at a rainbow. It might make a sickness in her finger. Thoughts of Hobah made her sad. She felt a great loneliness in this empty land.

The sheep were far from home, but now that night was cooling the air they moved a little faster.

A star was out before the little Bluebird reached the sandwash. Mother had come to meet her. Mother did not like to have her daughter far from her side. She helped the little Bluebird put the flock in for the night, and put the heavy bar across the gate of the night corral.

Then they went into the hogan. Father had gone to the Trading Post. He had gone for more silver for a concho belt he was making. Now he was home again. He was excited. He was happy. He was singing little bits of songs to himself. Mother and Doli heard him as they came around the hogan. They hurried. They knew something nice had happened.

When they came in, Father did not tell them. He tried to act as if nothing had happened. He tried to act as if this were like any other supper time. When Mother asked him where were the flour and baking powder she had told him to buy, he had to tell her he did not have them. He had forgotten to get them from the Trader. Mother just stood there, looking at him. Then Father had to tell her what had happened. He had to tell her what had made him forget the flour and the baking powder.

Hobah had written a letter from the School. Big Brother was there. He was working there for money. He was a good boy. Everybody liked him. Hobah was happy. She liked the School. All this had been in Hobah's letter. The Trader had read it to Father. Father showed the letter to Mother. He let Doli hold it.

Doli looked at the letter in her hand. Hobah liked the School and Hobah had seen Big Brother. Hobah was there at the same place with Big Brother. Perhaps she saw him every day. Perhaps she talked with him. Doli did not feel so happy about all this. She felt left out and hurt and alone. She felt jealous of the School that Hobah and Big Brother liked.

Mother and Father were looking at her. Father was talking. He seemed surprised that she was not listening. He had a package in his hand. He kept saying, "The Trader says it is for you. The Trader says your elder brother sent it. Take it, Small One. It is for you."

The package was a paper-covered box. It filled Doli's arms. Father helped her untie the string around it. He helped her take the paper off. He took the lid off. Inside was a doll.

Big Brother's gift was a doll. It was a doll with a white face and yellow hair. It had blue eyes. It was a White doll. It wore White Man's clothes and shoes and a bonnet. Doli was afraid of it. She would not touch it. She let it fall when Father handed it to her.

The family sat on the floor. They ate their supper. Father and Mother talked about Hobah and Big Brother, but Doli would not talk. She ate the good food that her mother had cooked because she was hungry, but she ate it in silence. She would not pick up the doll. She would not play with it. She would not touch it.

Father and Mother ate and talked. They did not look

at their little girl. They acted as if she were not there. Father said he hoped that Talking God was not around. He said that Talking God did not like bad children.

Doli finished her supper. She unrolled her sheepskin. She went to bed. She turned her face to the hogan wall.

The blue-eyed doll lay where it had fallen.

The next morning Doli got up when her mother called her. She ate her breakfast. She did not look at Big Brother's gift. She went to the corral and started the flock.

Today the sheep were not lazy. They hurried. They were restless. They reached the waterhole before the middle time of day.

There was no wind. The air was still and hot as if waiting for something. It was heavy.

By noon the sky had clouded. A yellow light moved in from the east. Wind started up in a great gust and blew in anger. The sky darkened. The wind died down and rain came. It came in a sheet of water pouring down on the little herder and her flock.

The arroyos, which had been but deep cracks in the hard-baked sand, now became full of rushing yellow water. A dull roar came with the rain, and lightning tore the sky and thunder tore the earth.

The sheep huddled wetly together. Doli did not know what to do.

Dusk was near before the rain stopped falling and only for a little while did Sun-Carrier show his face to give light to the rain-drenched land. Then he went to his western home and at once night came and filled the land.

No stars shone to light the home trail. Even Moon Mother was blanketed in darkness.

Hard rain fell steadily. Doli stumbled among the flock. The sheep turned this way and that way, crowding close to one another for warmth and protection. They were too frightened to know the way home. Doli was too frightened to lead them.

A flash of lightning showed two half-grown lambs near the edge of the flooded arroyo. Doli ran to them, but even as she reached out, clutching their wet wool with frightened hands, the arroyo bank gave way and the sheep fell into the angry waters. The force of the water whirled and turned the animals, dashing them against the steep sides and then playfully letting them up, atop the yellow foam. Doli ran along the arroyo brink above them. Their dumb sheep faces turned up to her for help. She leaned far over, trying to reach them, but the wild waters swept

them away from her. They were lost in the darkness.

It took Doli a long time, stumbling around in the rain and the night, to get back among her flock again. Then she sang to them for their comfort. She walked among them, singing the high sweet songs that a herder sings.

There Father found her, singing in the rain among the sheep. He held her close in his arms, close to his heart, his little Bluebird. He wrapped her in his blanket and started the flock homeward. Mother came panting up. She held a lantern high in her hand. She had been looking for her little girl. First of all she had to see that her little last one was safe in Father's arms. Then she righted the sheep. She walked among them and Father sang them along on the home trail to the safety and the shelter of the night corral.

When they reached the hogan, Mother blew on the fire coals to start them blazing. Father put his little girl close to the warmth of the blaze. Doli did not stay there. First she went across the hogan to pick up the blue-eyed doll from the floor. She placed a torn bit of blanket around it to cover the yellow hair. She put the doll near the fire. Then she went over to Mother to tell her that she had lost two of the half-grown lambs. Mother dried her child's wet hair. She took off her wet skirts and her soaking blouse, and the mud-stiffened moccasins. She gave her a bowl of hot mutton stew.

But before Doli tasted the food set before her, she put some of it aside for the white-faced doll.

She felt that she knew what had caused the cloudburst and the loss of two of the flock. Gifts given from the heart must be accepted by the heart. Evil comes to her whose thoughts are bad. She had allowed Big Brother's doll to fall to the floor. She had not played with it or touched it. She was glad that Big Brother had not been there to see the cloudburst. She hoped that he would never know how she had caused the rains to fall in anger.

White Doll slept near her that morning on Big Brother's sheepskin.

IX. THE NEW HOGAN

Uncle came with welcome news. He said he thought that Father needed a man to help him and so, Uncle said, he would come to help him. He would build a hogan for himself and his young wife near Mother's. They would spend the winter there. He said when the hogan was finished he would bring his horses over and his wagon and his saddle. He would drive their sheep over also, and herd them in with the family flock.

Doli was delighted. They would be company. They would be near all the time. She had forgotten that she had not liked the beautiful young girl that Uncle had married. She had forgotten that once she had mistrusted this young wife who had been to the School and was said to know so many things. She had forgotten this. She was happy now that they were coming.

Father was happy, too. He said he did need a young man around. There was a large flat place at the other end of the clearing from the juniper tree. Father said it was a good place for a hogan. He said it would be just the place for Uncle and his wife.

The men started building at once. First they had to go to the mountains for the right kind of trees for the logs of the hogan. That took a long time. Then the logs had to be cut the right lengths and peeled of their bark. Uncle said, "This hogan has to be a good one. It has to be just right or my wife will refuse to live in it." He said, "That's what the School does to them," but he laughed when he said it. He was proud of the School girl he had married. He was glad that she wanted nice things. He meant her to have them.

It took many days to build the hogan. It was larger

than Mother's. It had a window made of glass that Uncle bought at the Trader's. It had a store stove with a stove pipe. It had a wooden door. But it looked like Mother's with its rounded eight walls, its rounded roof, and its sanded floor. It looked just like Mother's, only larger.

When the hogan was finished and everything about it was just right, Uncle and his wife blessed it in the ancient way of the People.

They blessed it with Holy Song and prayer and pollen. Uncle sprinkled cornmeal around the outside of the hogan. He sang:

"May my house be blessed.
May it be holy.
May it be beautiful."

Uncle sprinkled cornmeal in the four directions and up and down. He sang:

"May it be blessed
From my heart to my feet
Where I lie and above me.
May it be beautiful beneath me.
May it be beautiful around me.
May it be blessed."

Uncle went inside the hogan. He sprinkled cornmeal on the floor and around the walls. He blew cornmeal upward. He sang as he walked about with the basket of sacred meal.

Then Uncle's wife came in. She kindled a fire in the stove in the middle of her hogan. Into its heart she threw cornmeal. She chanted softly:

"May it be delightful, my fire.
  May it give us warmth.
  May it give us light.
  May it be beautiful.
  May it be good,
  My fire, my holy fire."

The hogan blessed, Uncle's wife moved her possessions in from the wagon and began to keep her house.

She said to Doli, "Before the spring comes, I am going to have a sewing machine. I am going to buy it with my weaving money." Uncle's wife gave Doli a little pat. She said, "I will teach you to sew on the sewing machine, Little Sister." Doli's eyes grew big and black. Tears were in them. It was good to have Uncle and his beautiful wife live near them. Oh, it was good. It felt right.

After Uncle had moved all their possessions, he said he might as well herd all the sheep. He made a joke of it. He said he should be good for something, why not as a herder for the sheep? He said, "Let the little Bluebird stay at home now that winter comes near our red rocks."

Mother said she liked that. She smiled at Uncle as if she had known all the time why Father needed a man to help him.

The days grew shorter and colder. Wind blew sand in at the door and down the smoke hole.

Uncle's hogan was warmer and lighter than Mother's. Uncle's wife had her loom at one side. It was big enough for that. She said there was room enough for Mother's loom at the other side if she wanted it there. But Mother said no, although she came often to sit there by the window with her tow cards or her spindle.

Uncle's wife had dishes, white ones with a bluebird on them. She had a cupboard made of a box and covered with a curtain. She let Doli wipe the dishes and put them away in their cupboard house.

One day Uncle's wife talked of Hobah and Big Brother. At first, Doli could not listen. It made her heart bleed again, but finally she heard the words of the older girl.

Uncle's wife told of the everyday happenings of big Boarding School. She said that there were many boys and girls there. She said that all the children knew each other and liked each other and did things together. "Is it like a Sing?" Doli wanted to know. "Well, in some ways, yes, it is," the older girl answered. Then she went on to describe the buildings, the sleeping rooms, the playrooms, and the classrooms. She told of the work that Big Brother was probably doing, the things he was seeing. She spoke of Hobah and of the new ways she was learning, ways that were better because they would make Hobah stronger and happier.

Uncle's wife had liked going to School and she pictured it a happy and an exciting place to the little girl who knew nothing of the world beyond the sandwash.

Doli listened and it was not many days before she herself was saying, "Perhaps Big Brother is playing the ball game now," and, "Hobah will be surprised at this, when she comes home from School." "When Big Brother comes home this time, he can come to visit you so he can have a chair to sit on."

Father did not care for the new hogan. He said he was too old for such new kinds of things. He said Mother's place was much the better. So during the long autumn evenings, they all sat in Mother's hogan, before her fire, on her family's roll of sheepskins. Father and Uncle sang all the songs they knew. It seemed as if they could not get enough of singing.

Life was good. It was beautiful and good.

Doli leaned against her father's knee. She sang very softly a song of her own. She sang it for Mother and for Father, for Uncle and for his wife.

She sang:

"Oh, beautiful,
Oh, precious,
My family.
Oh, beautiful,
Oh, precious
My life,
My beautiful life."

X. LEARNING THINGS

Mother and Doli sat in the door of the hogan in the warm midday sun. Mother was telling her little girl things that it was time that she should know. They were talking about weaving and of designs for blankets. Mother said, "In the old days, I think, all designs had meanings. Every line was a symbol for something. That is what I think. But now many of those ancient meanings have been forgotten or perhaps new designs with no meanings have come into use. I myself use part of a design that my grandmother used. I put it some place in all my blankets, sometimes the way my grandmother gave it to me and sometimes I try it out in new ways."

Mother was quiet for a time, thinking of the old days when she was a little girl, even younger than the little Bluebird, when she was teasing her grandmother to teach her to weave. Those were goods days, Mother thought, easier than the life of today. Game was plentiful. There was more water, more rainfall, bigger rivers. Grass was better, too, in those days. She remembered places near her mother's hogan, where her oldest sister lived now, that used to have trees and high grass. It had nothing now. But then the People had enemies. There had been fighting nearly all of the time.

Mother looked down at the little girl sitting so patiently beside her. There would never be danger of this child's being carried off by an enemy in battle. The People had no enemies now.

Perhaps life was better now, after all; perhaps the

White world held good, some good for the children of
the People. The White Men were trying. They were trying
to bring back the water and the wild grass. Father had
told her, just the other day, how Washington was going
to pay the Indians to fill the arroyos on their land with
dirt. These arroyos were deep cuts in the earth that ate
away the grazing land and stole the rain waters, carrying
them away instead of letting them soak into the thirsty
sand. Mother sighed. She brought herself back to the
present. She continued her teaching.

With her fingers she drew symbols in the sand, explain-
ing the meanings for the ones she knew, mountains, clouds
and rain, whirlwind, rainbow and lightning.

Mother told Doli of the sacred meanings of color.

She pointed out red color. "That, Little One, is the
color of the setting sun. It is life color. It is strength."

Mother pointed to yellow. "It is the color of corn, the
life-giver. It is the color of harvest, of things grown to
ripeness."

Mother held up black yarn. "Black is of the north. It is
man color, having strength greater than woman strength.

"Browns and grays are for fulfillment. They mean
rounded endings. They mean finished.

"White is for the east. It is for the morning. It is for beauty.

"Green is for things growing. It is for increasing life."

· Mother gave blue yarn to her listening child. "Blue is your color. It is goodness. It is happiness. It is gentleness. It knows but one trail, the straight one. Follow your color, my child, as the bluebird flies."

A wind stirred the sleeping day. Doli dreamed of the things that might come to her, as she sat in the bright sunshine before the hogan door.

Doli could not card the wool. It took strong hands for carding, but she tried. She could get almost all the knots out. "Hands grow stronger by their need for being strong," her mother told her. Her mother's spindle was a little long and a little heavy for the small brown hands, but Mother said that was the way to learn. Mother said, "The People learn by doing." She said, "Do things with what you have to do them with."

Doli and Uncle's wife liked to dye yarns even more than Mother did. Mother was always afraid she could not match the colors. She was always a little cross at dyeing time. Mother did things quickly and by guess. Uncle's wife was not so sure. She had to weigh and measure. She was much slower. She had to figure things out before she started. That was the way they had taught her to do at School.

Father and Uncle had long talks about which way was better. Father thought that Mother's way was better, but Uncle was not so sure.

Mother spun enough yarn at one time for what she thought would do her blanket. Then she took it to the well. She threw a little dye into a bucket, about what she thought would be enough. She poured water in and boiled the dye and the yarn together. They were always good colors when they came out, but sometimes when Mother was trying to match a color it did not match. That made Mother cross, but she used it anyway.

Almost always Mother was right about how much yarn she needed, but sometimes she did not have enough to finish her blanket.

Uncle's wife worked by making numbers with a pencil on white paper for a long time before she started spinning her yarn. That way showed her how much she needed to spin, but sometimes her numbers did not tell her right and then, like Mother, she had to spin some more.

Uncle's wife was slower at dyeing, too. She took more

trouble. She weighed everything. She had a little scale.
Everything had to be just right before she put her yarns
in the dye water.

Uncle's wife wanted to dye with plant colors. She
always was trying some new plant to see what color it
would give. Mother bought her dye in little paper packages from the Trader, but sometimes, when she was not
too busy, she tried the different kinds of plants. Plant
colors were softer and more beautiful than store dyes.
Uncle said they brought a better price at the Trader's,
too. He was always bringing home some new plant for
his wife to try. Some of them made lovely colors. Some of
them the sun would fade, but others were "fast colors."

Uncle's wife knew how to use indigo to make blue, but
she was always hunting for some plant of the red rock
country that would make blue, also. Uncle hunted every
day while he was herding the sheep and at night he would
have little bunches of withered plants and flowers to be
boiled and tested, but they never made blue. Father said
he thought some kind of rock might make it and Mother
said she had heard there was a blue clay that could be
used for dye.

When it came time for Doli to learn to weave, Uncle

made her a small loom that could be put up near her
mother's. Mother did not like that. She said she had learned
on her mother's and her grandmother's looms, weaving
on their blankets. Uncle just laughed. He said times had
changed. He said the little Bluebird should have her own
small loom. Father brought Big Brother's sheepskin out
for her to sit upon.

Mother showed her how to string the loom with warp
threads. She showed her how to use the batten, how to
turn it to make it hold the warp strings apart, how to run
the yarn through it and beat it hard into place.

Doli wove upward, sitting on Big Brother's sheepskin. She wove upward as far as her slender arms could reach, then Mother showed her how to loosen the web and roll it and sew it, even though it was a small one, and begin again.

Doli wove a stripe design. She planned to make one stripe for every member of her family. In between were white stripes because Mother had said, "White is for beauty."

The blanket grew slowly on the small loom that stood so proudly near the large one in the clearing by the juniper tree.

At last it was finished. Doli sat on her feet and looked at it a long time before she went to find her mother to tell her the news.

Mother took it off the loom and they washed it clean with sand.

That night Doli put it on the floor of the hogan for everyone to look at. The edges were a little tight. It was a little out of shape. Its stripes were a little crooked, but it was a good blanket to look at. Everyone said so.

The next morning Mother, Father, and Doli went to the Trading Post. They went to see their friend the Trader.

Doli wanted to ask him something. All the way to the Trading Post her heart thumped excitedly at what she wanted to ask the Trader.

When they got there, Mother traded her blanket for money and for food and Father traded the concho belt he had made for money and some boots which he needed for winter. Doli waited for them to finish. She felt like a big girl now, for was she not carrying her first blanket rolled in a tight bundle beneath her store shawl?

At last Mother and Father were through trading. The Trader came from behind the counter. He came to speak to the little Bluebird and to give her candy as he always did. Doli pulled aside her blanket and drew her roll of weaving. Shyly she showed it to the Trader. He held it up. He looked at it. He counted the seven colored stripes and the eight white ones. It was not so very crooked. It was almost beautiful.

The Trader liked it. He wanted to buy it. He went to get the money but Doli told him no. The Trader asked her if she wanted to take it back again to the hogan. Doli said no. Her heart beat faster than ever. Now she must tell him what she wanted to do with the blanket. She opened her mouth, but no words came. The Trader asked her if she wanted to leave the blanket with him for a while, not to sell it, but just to loan it. But this, too, brought the answer no. They were talking in Navajo.

Then the Trader waited quietly. He knew that Doli would tell him what she wanted just as soon as she could make the words come. He waited. Mother and Father waited. They did not know. They could not help her tell the Trader. She had not told them.

A wasp buzzed around the store. He almost got on the Trader's bald head. The Trader jumped and slapped at the wasp. It made Doli laugh to see the Trader be so frightened of a wasp. Then she stood on tiptoe. She told the Trader very low, she told him what she wanted him to do with her blanket. She wanted him to send it to Big Brother. She wanted it to be a message to call him home.

The Trader took her behind the counter. He let her sit on the counter to watch him while he wrote the letter. He pretended that Doli could read what he was writing. Every little while he would ask her, "Is that the way I should say it? Is that telling him right?"

Then he wrapped the blanket. Doli helped him tie it with a strong cord. She stood on tiptoe in the corner that was the Post Office of the Trading Post. She licked the stamps that went on the package. She helped to push it in the leather bag that the mail carrier took.

It took a long time, but it was important. It was right that time should be spent in getting it done.

Going home, Doli sat on the wagon seat between her father and her mother. Father did not sing. Mother did not talk. Doli did not ask to help drive the horses. Everyone was silent, busy with his own thoughts, but it was a happy silence.

It was a good and happy silence that went along with them back to the hogan from the Trading Post.

XI. WINTER

Cold weather was on its way. The rattlesnakes had gone
to sleep. The horses were putting on their woolly coats.
There was frost in the air.

Father had heard at the Trading Post that the winter
would be a hard one and a long one, for it was said that
the Hast-sezini dancers had danced without their masks
and the Anaye were angry.

In the Chuska Mountains piñons were plentiful. Father decided that the family would go there to gather a winter's supply of nuts. They had told him at the Post that the piñon crop was the largest that it had been in seven years. The Trader said he would buy all that Father would have to sell. Father was eager to start.

Uncle and his wife both wanted to go, but someone had to stay with the sheep. Finally it was decided that Uncle would stay at home. On the way to the mountains Father would stop at the hogan of Mother's oldest sister to see if her largest boy would come to relieve Uncle. If he could come, then Uncle would ride his pony to catch up with the family wagon.

The ride to the Chuskas in the wagon was not a pleasant one. Father had put on the canvas wagon top and Mother and Uncle's wife had brought all their blankets and sheepskins. But the wind blew bitterly cold for so early in winter. The canvas flapped at every icy gust and the blankets could not keep out all the cold.

There was too much wind to make a proper campfire and what food was eaten was uncooked and cold.

The campsite in the Chuskas was finally reached. Many families were camping there. Rude shelters of piñon and cedar had been built and wagons and horses and campfires were clustered among the trees.

Father hastened to put up his shelter before the short cold day came to an end. When he had finished, he and Mother blessed it as if it were a hogan. This done, Uncle's wife unpacked the cooking pots and cooked the evening meal.

In the morning the family began picking piñons. As long as daylight lasted, men, women, and children picked the small brown nuts. Navajo blankets and squares of canvas were put on the ground under the trees and small boys shook down the piñon nuts. Frequently a whole cone would come tumbling down on someone's head. Then there would be laughter and haste to see if the cone had spilled its supply of nuts on the waiting blanket. Pack rat and squirrel nests were robbed. This last method gave the most nuts in the shortest time and for the least work.

The piles of nuts on the blankets and squares of canvas grew rapidly into little hills. It was a good year for piñons.

Uncle arrived. On the way he had shot a deer and so there was feasting and song and story telling around the warmth of the night fires.

Several days went by. Father and his family were almost ready to return home, but the camp was so gay and the nuts so plentiful that he decided to stay a little longer. A few families left, but most of them thought as Father did. The piñon crop was better than it had been for years. Everyone was happy. There was great merriment among the pickers.

Then snow began to fall. It came much earlier than the People had expected. For two days and nights it fell with deadly stillness. Everything was covered with a blanket of white. Snow came up to the wagon beds. It was heavy, firmly packed, crusted, and water-filled. Some of the bough shelters caved in under the weight of snow upon their tops. Dry wood for fires was hard to find. Food gave out. There was nothing to eat but what the men were able to supply in game.

During this bitter time one of the women in the next camp became ill. She coughed deeply and her eyes were bright with fever. Uncle told his wife about her. He said her family had moved out. Navajos are afraid of sickness. He said the woman was in there alone.

Uncle's wife said at once that she would go to her. Mother told her not to go. She said it was not right that she should go. Uncle's wife said she was not afraid. She

said at School they had taught her differently. She set about preparing things to take with her to the woman's camp. She tore up a clean skirt into smooth squares. She got out a box of matches that she had hidden somewhere.

Mother watched her getting ready. Uncle's wife did not hurry, although she could hear the sick woman's deep coughing. She counted the things she had, clean rags, a box of matches, a pot of mutton stew, a bottle of "Gov'ment" medicine. It was not much, but it was all she had. She put them in a flour sack. She drew her blanket closer around her and, pulling the boughs aside, stooped to go through the doorway.

Then Mother spoke to her. She told her to wait. She said, "We go together."

When they reached the next shelter, they found the sick woman burning with fever. She was weak with hunger and filled with the terror of illness alone. The women cared for her as best they could.

Father stayed with Doli in their shelter of boughs. They played clapping games. Father taught her a dance step. It was better to keep moving.

Mother came back for dry wood. Her face was gray

and Doli knew that it was caused by fear. It was too much for the little girl. She began to cry. She could hear the sick woman, the world was so stilled with falling snow. Her mother spoke to her sharply, "Are you a baby? Perhaps you need a cradle-board." Doli was ashamed, but now that the tears had started she could not seem to stop them. She, too, was weak from hunger and cold and fright. She lay huddled on the floor of the shelter, sobbing and crying.

Night came and the snow continued to fall. The wind came up to blow the snow in great drifts. Uncle had gone wading through the snow drifts to a camp farther on where there was said to be a Medicine Man. Mother had sent him. Uncle's wife had done for the sick woman all that she knew how to do.

Death was coming for the woman.

Uncle did not come back. There was no fire in the bough shelter now. Mother had taken the dry wood. Father made Doli stand up. He rubbed her face, her hands, her feet. He made her walk with him around and around the narrow floor space in the bough shelter.

Snow fell steadily, mercilessly, blanketing life.

Just before gray dawn lighted the snow-filled air,

Uncle came back with the Medicine Man. It was too late. Death had come for the woman.

Mother and Uncle's wife came back. Uncle's wife looked tired. Mother's face was closed. Her eyes looked straight ahead, telling nothing. She opened her blanket; there, close to her heart, was a small wrapped bundle.

Uncle came in with dry wood. He had found some, somewhere. He made a fire. It blazed upward in the cold shelter. It lighted the darkness. It warmed the chill. It made things friendlier and warmer.

Mother unwrapped the bundle. It was a baby.

Father was troubled. He said, "If the mother is not here among us now, perhaps . . ." but Mother would not let him finish. She said to Uncle's wife, "You seem to have learned many useful and many wise things in the School where they sent you. It may be, as you say, that this child should be one of us. We shall learn if this that you say is true, for I am keeping this baby." Mother looked at Father. He did not speak again, but he still looked troubled. He had been taught that death was harmful to those who were living. He had been taught that it was unwise to keep a new baby whose mother had died. The new ways of the White School confused Father.

He did not understand them. He did not approve of them. But even as he disapproved he looked shyly at the baby. Father loved babies. Perhaps Uncle's wife knew best. He would wait before he spoke again.

The Medicine Man, whom Uncle had brought, sang Holy Songs for the two women who had stayed where death had been. He prayed for them and performed holy acts for their good. He sang Holy Songs for the new baby and sprinkled it with sacred pollen. Then he sang for Doli and for Father and for Uncle, as they had been near those who had stayed where death had been. It took a long time to do this, for everything must be done in a certain way just as it always had been done. Nothing must be changed or left out or hurried.

At last the Medicine Man had finished. He had done all that he knew how to do. He felt certain that evil and harm had been frightened away and only good remained.

Father paid him for his work with piñons and Uncle paid him with a blanket and a basket and a promise of some sheep. The Holy Man went away. Other people were calling for him. He was wanted in many places, for it was a time of suffering and sorrow.

Another dawn filled the world. Sun-Carrier struggled

through the snow clouds. Father took the new baby in his arms. If he still had fear of this young thing it did not show in his eyes or in his face or in his ways with it. Other people might fear the new one. Other people might stay as far as they could from Mother's shelter for a time, but they would forget. After a while they would forget. It was a time of death. Many families would have been touched by the same evil.

Father smiled tenderly at the baby in his arms. Uncle smiled at his young wife as if to tell her, "You are doing well by your loved School for you are sharing its wisdom with many."

Father sang the baby song which welcomed this new one to this middle-world. He held the baby to the east and his high voice sent music to all the piñon camps.

Father sang:

"The Early Dawn found a baby,
   To the east it found a baby."

Father held the baby to the south. He sang:

"The Sun Ray Girl found a baby,
   To the south she found a baby."

Father held the baby to the west. He sang:

"Yellow Dawn Boy found a baby,
 To the west he found a baby."

Father held the baby to the north. He sang:

"North Star found a baby,
 To the north it found a baby."

Father held the baby upward to the above-world.
Mother sprinkled it with pollen. Then Uncle's wife
reached for the baby. It was blue with cold. She warmed
cloths and wrapped the baby in them. She gave it water,
drop by drop on the tip of her finger.

Day passed. The snow had stopped, the wind died
down, but the air grew colder. All day Uncle's wife sat
with the baby by the fire, rubbing it, wrapping it in
warmed cloths, giving it drops of water. Doli knelt beside her. She held the baby when the older girl became
too tired.

Uncle kept the fire blazing. He kept bringing in sticks
of dry wood. Where he got them, Doli did not know.

By night the baby was still alive. Its little blue body
still breathed. Mother took turns with Uncle's wife.

Father went out to find more wood. Doli slept, wrapped in her shawl, on the floor between the fire and the baby.

Then help came.

On every reservation for Indians there are men appointed by the Government whose duty it is to help Indians at all times. These men are called Agency Superintendents.

The day before, word of the Navajos' danger had reached their Agency Superintendent. At once he had called far and wide for White people to come aid him in rescuing the Indians.

On horseback and by automobile and tractors the White Men reached the Indians' camp. They fought their way into the snow-filled canyons. They brought horses and food and hope to the penned-in People.

The Red Cross chartered an airplane which like a giant bird circled far over the tree tops trying to sight the piñon camp. Then Uncle's wife did a wonderful thing. She waded out through the snow drifts to a flat place where there were no trees. She made marks in the snow with a piñon bough. The marks were words in English. They said, "WE ARE HERE. DROP FOOD HERE." The "Giant Bird" dropped food in packages.

Doli saw the "Giant Bird" as she stood holding the tiny baby hard to her body.

The People were saved. Father's family reached home again, only this time there was a new one with them. This time there was a baby in Mother's hogan. There was someone for Doli to care for, to play with, and to love.

They were home for many days before Father went to the Trading Post. He needed to go and so did Uncle, but staying at home had felt so good that they had not liked to leave. Finally Uncle's wife said Uncle had to go. She needed things from the Post. So he and Father went.

When they came back, Father had a letter for Doli. Uncle's wife read it to them while Mother made fried bread for supper. It was from Hobah and Big Brother. They had written it together. It had news. Sometime, the letter said, between lambing time and shearing time, they were coming home. They were coming home together and they would stay all through the long days of summer. Maybe, if Big Brother could get work with the CCC, he would stay at home. It was time, he wrote, that he married and made a home. At the bottom of the page the letter said, "It was your blanket, Little Bluebird, that called me to come home."

Doli took the letter to bed with her that night. She carried it around with her for days. Uncle's wife taught her to read it. Doli said, "When I go to School I am . . ." and then she looked at Uncle's wife. She was surprised at what she said. Last year when she was smaller she had said she was never going to School. Well, that was last year. She was bigger now.

She and Uncle's wife talked much together. They talked of The Baby, what to do for it. How much it grew! They talked of Elder Sister and Big Brother. They talked of School. Doli could not forget that it had been

Uncle's wife who had known how to write the words in the snow for the "Giant Bird" to see. She knew that School had taught her that. School had saved the People.

Winter began in the canyons and the valleys and in the shelter of the red rocks.

Winter wind blew and snow fell, but inside the hogans it was warm and light. There were song and laughter.

All was beautiful and good.

XII. THE NIGHT CHANT

Father came home with news. There was to be a Night
Chant at a hogan four miles on the other side of the Trading Post. He talked with Mother about it. Later he talked
with Uncle and Mother talked with Uncle's wife. They
seemed happy and pleased about something.

Uncle's wife finished the blanket she was weaving. She and Uncle went to the Trading Post. When they returned they had many bundles and sacks. They ate their evening meal at Mother's hogan. Uncle talked a lot and laughed a lot. Hardly had food been finished before he and Father began to sing.

Doli put the supper things away. She brought in an armful of wood for Mother's fire. Then she sat by Uncle's wife and watched Father sing to the baby. The baby was brown and fat now. He had thick black hair all over his round little head. He had round black eyes. He was getting two chins. Uncle called him Little-Hides-Behind-His-Chins, but Doli did not think much of that name. Father called him Son and that was better. Mother and Uncle's wife just said "The Baby" all the time.

Now Uncle's wife untied her packages. She had bought blue flannel and pink flannel for dresses for The Baby. She had bought a baby blanket and cotton and vaseline. Mother and Father were interested in the things she had bought. Father was making a cradle-board and a bracelet for his son. Pink and blue dresses were all right, he said, but after all a cradleboard and a silver bracelet were things that Navajo babies had to have.

After a while The Baby went to sleep and it was Uncle's turn to hold him. Uncle made jokes at The Baby, that was his way, but he liked him just as much as anyone.

Father called his little Bluebird to his side. He looked at her gravely. All the others were quiet. Doli's heart began to beat faster. She felt excited. Something big was going to happen.

Then Father began to speak. He spoke slowly and low. His words were heavy with meaning. He told the little Bluebird about the Yei, about the under-world and the middle-world and the above-world.

Then he told her something else. She was to go with the family to the Night Chant, the sacred ceremony of the People. But that was not all. There was to be something else.

This year she was old enough to see the Gods. She was to take part in that ceremony where the children of the People see for the first time the People's Gods.

This year she was to see the Talking God, Grandfather of all the Gods. Doli was frightened. She was not sure she wanted to see the Gods. Father told her she was to see them. She was old enough.

Then Uncle's wife got out the biggest bundle that she

had brought home from the Trading Post. Mother and she untied it. There was yellow calico with tiny red flowers. There was brown calico with red and yellow dots. There were four cards of green braid and a little twist of yellow braid. That was for the skirts. There were blue velvet and orange sateen. They were for the blouse.

At first, Doli could not believe that they were for her, but Mother said they were. Uncle's wife said she would make them, but—and she laughed over at Doli as she said it, as if they had a joke about it—"I will have to have a sewing machine for these, I think."

Uncle laughed too. He said, "Is the sewing machine at

the Day School broken?" His wife just looked at him. So Uncle said quickly, "I think the Trader will buy that brown colt of mine. Maybe he will. I could get the sewing machine and if I hold out long enough some money besides, I think."

Doli could not sleep that night. She was frightened because she was to see the Gods. She was pleased because she was to have new clothes. She was excited about the sewing machine. She remembered that Uncle's wife had said she would have one before the summer. Doli wondered if Uncle's wife would teach her to use it. She thought she would. It was all too much. It kept sleep away.

Father went with Uncle the next morning to trade the brown colt. He thought he could help Uncle drive a good bargain. They were gone two days, but when they returned the sewing machine was in the back of Father's wagon. There was a new store blanket for Doli to wear. Father had traded some silver for it and for some turquoise to make her a necklace and bobs for her ears.

The sewing machine was wonderful. Uncle's wife knew how to make it go. She knew what all the wheels were for. Mother cut out the dress for Doli and Uncle's wife sewed it. It was wider than the old skirt. It had deeper ruffles and two rows of braid. The blouse was beautiful. The orange sateen lining showed just a little at the neck, down the front, and on the sleeves. Father brought in a bag of silver buttons and Mother put them in rows on the front of the blouse and from the wrists to the elbows on the sleeves.

Uncle made beaded armbands. He put silver bells on her belt fringe. He put new soles on her moccasins.

Doli was busy and excited, but through it all Father took time and Uncle took time to talk with her of holy things. She was set apart. She was treated with respect for she would see the Gods. She was to stand before them in the ceremony. She was to hear them speak. She was to see them.

The day drew near for the beginning of the Night Chant. Mother's oldest sister's largest boy came over to herd the sheep. He said all his family but his younger brother were going to the Night Chant. He said they had heard that Doli was to be among the People who were to see the Gods. He said when he was older he would see them. He said he would not be frightened, but he said it a little doubtfully. He knew in his heart that he would be.

There were hundreds of Navajos gathered for the great Night Chant. A large medicine hogan had been built for the ceremony. Nearer the hogan of Hasteen Begay, who

was having the chant, were cookshades made of evergreen branches standing upright.

Dawn Singer was there. He patted the head of the little Bluebird. He seemed to remember her.

Mother washed Doli's hair in yucca suds. She put her new dress on her. Between the silver buttons she pinned safety pins to make it even prettier.

The Night Chant began with the sprinkling of corn pollen, with song and dancing, with ceremony and feast-ing.

On the fifth night the children who were to see the Gods were called into the ceremonial hogan. There were two

small boys and two small girls. Their heads were bowed. Their eyes were hidden by their blankets. They were led in. Somewhere there was the sound of soft drumming. There were cries of "Hu-hu-hu-hu," the holy cry.

Cedar smoke made the air smell sweet. There was holiness in the ceremonial hogan. Doli could feel it although she could not see; her eyes were covered. They were standing before the Gods. She felt it in the wild beating of her heart, in the frightened feeling in her throat, in the shaking of her knees.

In a moment more someone would tell her to drop her blanket. Someone would tell her to raise her eyes. Then she would see them. Then she would be different from what she was now for she would have seen the Gods.

The boys were led to the back of the hogan. The girls were led to one side. The Gods put pollen on the small boys and struck them with a yucca leaf. The Gods touched the small girls with spruce tips and corn ears. They cried, "Hu-hu-hu-hu," the holy cry.

It was a holy place. Doli felt it. Doli knew it. She was standing before the Gods.

Then came the low-voiced order, "Drop your blankets. Raise your eyes and behold the Gods."

Doli did as she was told to do. Her blanket slid from her shoulders and fell in a little pool of bright colors about her feet. She raised her head.

She saw the Gods. She saw them in a line facing her. She saw them. Now and forever she would be a true daughter of the People. She had seen the Gods.

The ceremony went on. Other things were done that were a part of it.

Doli was not frightened now. She looked under her long eyelashes at the small boys and the other small girl. She

smiled at the other girl. She was not at all frightened now.

Doli felt older. She felt brave and strong. There were gladness and singing in her heart.

When it was over and she was outside again, she found her mother and her father. They took her hands. They were looking at her and at each other. They were happy and proud.

Then Father turned away to chant the great prayer of the People.

"In the house of life I wander
  With beauty before and behind me,
  With beauty above and below me,
  With beauty within and around me
  To old age traveling
  On the beautiful trail of life."

Father went away somewhere, but Mother stood beside her Little Last One. Mother's hand swiftly touched her small girl's hair. Mother's gentle voice came softly, "Follow your trail as the bluebird flies."

Doli looked up at this woman who always had been her friend and her guide. "My Mother, I am wondering if the bluebird flies into the white man's world." Quickly the older woman answered her, "The bluebird knows no world. It knows only that its wings are strong enough to take it where its heart directs."

"My wings are strong, my Mother, and I have listened to the calling of my heart." Doli's mother turned away. She drew her blanket up about her face, but through its muffled folds her voice came clearly. "We must go home, my child. There are so many things I must teach you before you go away to the School."

Doli walked along beside her mother. Quietly she walked along, but deep within she was singing, "I am going to School. I am going to School. I will follow my trail as the bluebird flies."